Lighthouse Community

Charter School's Anthology:

Freedom to Express

Foreword by Rev. Matthew Fox, Ph.D.,
Founder of Y.E.L.L.A.W.E. - A Creative Arts Youth Program

authorHOUSE®

AuthorHouse™
1663 Liberty Drive
Bloomington, IN 47403
www.authorhouse.com
Phone: 1-800-839-8640

First published by AuthorHouse:05/26/09

ISBN: 978-1-4389-8978-5 (sc)

Printed in the United States of America
Bloomington, Indiana

This book is printed on acid-free paper.

Cover art by Hector Ramirez, 12th grade

Contents

12th Grade Entries

Acknowledgements

I am in awe of and deeply moved by the first graduating class of Lighthouse Community Charter School. This small group of talented and passionate students is in the process of transitioning from high school to college or the career of their choice. They have committed themselves to their education and lives so powerfully that I was inspired to create a way to show tribute to them. But what would be the best way to honor them and highlight their incredible talents? I had the privilege of meeting Barbara Tavres, Community Relations Manager of Barnes and Noble Booksellers, Jack London Square branch. She presented me with the opportunity to publish this book. This was the perfect solution, because the students could leave Lighthouse as published authors. Barbara also connected me with Matthew Fox and Marlin Foxworth. Matthew agreed to write the Foreword for our book. Matthew's words are eloquent and poignant, providing a broader context to this project. I believe Marlin agreed to write an endorsement for our book out of his commitment to education and providing creative ways for students to express themselves. Barbara you are generous, resourceful and kind, bless you for this opportunity. Thanks to each of you for your contributions.

This book was created through collaboration. My partners were Drea Beale, 11th grade Humanities teacher and Yael Irom, 12th grade Humanities teacher. They were easy and flexible to work with which helped to make working on this project an enjoyable experience. I am in gratitude to both of them for their dedication to the completion of this book.

Lighthouse Community Charter School is a family. We choose to relate to each other through our 10 Guiding Principles: Collaboration, Communication, Compassion, Courage, Curiosity, Integrity, Reflection, Respect, Responsibility and Persistence. Integrating these principles into our language and our culture provides us with a context for miracles to happen every day. This anthology is one of those miracles. Another miracle is that beginning in the Fall of 2009 we will come together as a K-12 community, no longer being housed on two campuses. This is truly a dream come true!

I am excited for you to read the students' work and experience the world through their eyes. I believe you too will be awed, inspired and deeply moved by the unique ways these students expressed themselves.

By Janet Y. Tillman, Dean of Students

For more information about Lighthouse Community Charter School please visit:
www.lighthousecharter.org

Foreword

To write, to commit to print, to make poetry, to tell stories, to create DVD's and film, to take photography—all creative expression is a form of healing. It heals the soul of the individual and it heals the greater community. Indeed, when art is not doing its work of healing it is probably not art—it is more an ego trip or a fame trip—one thing that makes art such a powerful a force for healing is that it comes from wounds, whether one's own or those of the culture at large or, as is usually the case, from both at once. Art also heals because it creates pride and self-awareness in the artist and an "a ha!" in the recipient of the art. Art helps distinguish oneself as an individual and not just one sheep in a herd of other sheep. One takes a stand in one's art. One stands up and is counted. One draws a line whether writing or painting, dancing or sculpting, making film or making choreography.

Reading the poems and reflections in this collection was a moving experience for me. So many diverse topics and themes, all of which are universal. You can be sixteen and experience heartbreak or fear or love or tears—or you can be seventy-six and experience the same. These poems, written by teenagers, bear witness to the universality of life and its challenges. Young or old, we are in this together. The advice given: "Don't let the drugs win"; "Stop!"; "Don't judge"; "Rest and look at the sky smiling at you!"; "Going to college can be a sacrifice"; "It's imperative to get tested"—it all rings true. Sage and wise advice. There is plenty of wisdom on these pages. Poems are soothing. Art is revealing. It uncloaks our souls, their struggles and their triumphs. Art is not about age. It is about the naked truth and there is much naked truth in these pages.

Art is full of choices, as life is, or morality. All ethics is about making choices. All art is about making choices—what color, what note, what beat, what word, what image, what size, what length, what editing, what message—the options go on and on. Learning to live with options and choosing wise ones, all this is learned in art also. So too it is hard work. Whether practicing the piano or getting a painting just right, whether writing, researching, editing and re-editing an essay, whether getting the lighting right and the images right and the sound right and then the editing right in film-making—all of it takes time and commitment, sweat and tears and money-raising too. All of it is demanding and tests one's intentions, indeed purifies them.

Art also arouses praise. It turns people on. It gets us into states of awe and wonder, of beauty and gratitude. It moves us. It awakens our capacity for seeing truth in its many variations and diverse expressions, in different colors and rhymes and words and images and cadences and scenes and emotions and more. It expands our souls and it also awakens them and calls forth their intrinsic desire to say: "Yes!" or "Why didn't I say that?" or "Isn't that beautiful?" or "I must remember this" or "Thank God for that insight" and much more.

And for the artist there is a deep satisfaction that "I have spoken my truth." "I have said something I had to say and in a way that speaks to the imagination of others." All this is behind the work of art and artists.

For all these reasons and more, it is a privilege for me to be asked to respond to young peoples' art as found in these pages. The ensuing essays demonstrate that true art comes from the wounds of culture and of individuals for the writers here, though young, are not innocent. They have not emerged into the throes of adolescence without wounds, wounds from their families, from the streets, from their peers, from society at large, from life itself. But they are doing something about their wounds in these pages. They are naming them. They are opening the eyes of others to them. They are yelling them out. That is why this book is a healing book and those writing in it are healers as they also develop their craft as artists.

May we who read these stories and poems be artists ourselves in discerning how healing can happen in us and in society thanks to the gift of these young and aspiring, bold and inspiring voices. May praise follow. Not just praise of these artists and their truth-telling but praise of existence itself, praise that instructs us that, whatever the depth of the wounds we take on, being invited to join the caravan of human and cosmic history is still a thing of beauty and wonder and gratitude and amazement. For that reason we praise.

By Matthew Fox, Author

Rev. Matthew Fox is a Scholar in Residence for The Academy for the Love of Learning and the founder of Y.E.L.LA.W.E (Youth & Elders Learning Laboratory for Ancestral Wisdom Education), which is a creative arts youth program. He is also the author of 29 books including his most recent, "The A.W.E. Project: Reinventing Education, Reinventing the Human", "Original Blessing" and "Creativity: Where the Divine and the Human Meet." For more information please visit: www.yellawe.org

6TH GRADE ENTRIES

We started this poetry unit last year towards the beginning of 5th grade. The project commenced with studying a modified version of Georgia Heard's "Awakening the Heart". During this time we drew our hearts and labeled the things we live and fight for. These varied greatly, from peace, to our families, languages, and taking care of the environment. Throughout this process students were able to identify various aspects of their culture and what makes them a community. From that point we delved into a poetry genre study exploring the organization, rhythms, figurative language, and inspirations of other poets. We used various found poems to inspire our writing and eventually chose one seed piece to take through the writing process. The following are a few examples of poetry that we created. They represent our Guiding Principles ranging from compassion, to curiosity, persistence, and reflection. On behalf of the current 6th graders, please enjoy.

By Wanda Watson, 6th grade Humanities teacher

Don't Judge

By Jose M. Arteaga
6th grade

Don't judge.
Everybody is the same.
Sometimes we have different races or languages.
Sometimes we have different skin colors.

We are still the same.
Do people think we are different on the outside or the inside?
We are all human, right?
So, please don't judge.

We might come from different places.
But we are still the same.
We might have other traditions.
But we are still the same.
So, don't judge.
Please don't judge.

Me and Space!

By Estefania Avila
6th grade

Me and space are friends.
I read stories about it.
I want to be an astronaut.
I heard that it is fun.
Me and space!

I went to Mercury.
It was so hot that we could cook cold food on the ground.
Then I went to Pluto.
It was so small that it looks like a ball of ice, metal, and rock.
I went to the moon.
There are humps all around.
It looks like a broken street in the middle of Oakland.

Stop!

By Genesis Bustamante
6th grade

Stop child abuse
Stop deportation
Stop abortion
Stop making nonsense things

Policeman killing
Violence
Selling drugs
Got to go

Stop killing innocents
Stop killing to be respected
Stop killing for money
Stop splitting families
Stop!
Stop!!
Stop!!!

Stop separating and start supporting families

Don't Fall In!

By Diego Cardenas
6th grade

I know it's hard, I know it's difficult.
I know it's damaging, but please stop:
the violence,
the drugs, the drinking, and
the bad gangs that are only causing lives to be lost.

Please do stop because you are only hurting yourself.
Please do stop if you are hoping to live much longer.
Please do stop before it's too late.

Don't let the drugs beat you to a pulp.
Don't let the drugs win, because trust me,
I know you are stronger.
All I ask of you is to fight.
Don't let yourself be defeated!

What is Love?

By Samantha Ceja
6th grade

Love is like
a juicy apple
you cannot let go of.

Love is beautiful
like a sunset going down.

A kiss is like a piece of butter
on your cheek.
A kiss is sweet like a lollipop.

A hug is loving
A hug is nice.

Love
Hugs
Kisses

Destruction on Earth

By Adrian Lopez Luna
6th grade

Destruction on earth is like
my head blowing up when
I can't handle anymore because
people are fighting too much

Destruction on earth is like war
going on in front of me
and me seeing everything disappear
with a big loud Boom!

Destruction on earth is like war going on in front of me
and me seeing everyone die
everywhere around me
When will it end?
I just want to rest from the
destruction on earth

Nature

By Kellsy Nava
6th grade

If there wasn't any nature
then there wouldn't be any peace
and quiet for people.

Life would be like a hive with
bees everywhere!
Life will be like an anthill with
ants crawling everywhere!

If there wasn't any nature,
there wouldn't be any countries,
towns or even villages.

Cars and buildings would
be looking at you all of the time
no space to rest and look
at the sky smiling at you!

What If...

By Ricky Noel
6th grade

What if the world were like a video game?
You might have a controller.
You can make yourself go anywhere.

What if the world were like a video game?
You could go to school just by pressing a button.

What if the world were like a video game?
You could skip days…
Or skip to different places.

What if the world were like a video game?
You could make a car or plane appear right in front of you.
You could do whatever you wanted as long as everything was like a videogame!!!

…and remember you can always use cheat codes if you get stuck!!!

Invincible

By Kimberly Sotelo
6th grade

I can float into space without a space suit.
I am invincible.
I am as strong as metal, if I get hit, it won't hurt me!
I am invincible.

I've been climbing and moving in my dreams.
I am invincible.
Once you know me, you won't hurt me!
I am invincible.

Won't you give me a break?
You can't hurt me!
I am invincible.
I won't stop walking.
I won't stop walking.

I am invincible.

I Cry

By Nancy Vuong
6th grade

I will cry if my parents die
I cry when someone special gets hurt
I cry when no one cares

Crying is a million raindrops falling from a gray cloud feeling as if it can't stop
It makes you feel sad and unwanted

People walking by afraid to say, "Hi" to someone who's sad and needs a friend

But they don't care; they're just scared to help someone who's not their friend

Understand

By Wanda Watson
6th grade Humanities teacher

If I could leave you with only one message
It would be: Hold on to your love
Let it guide your thoughts, actions, and pursuits
Because when we lose our sense of love
Our soul is restless, hurt, and lost

Hold on to your love
Because intelligence without love
Leaves you cynical, angry, and mad
Have something to look forward to
Even when the oppression gets too heavy
Stay comforted by the genuine tenderness you feel
When you love, are loved, and believe in love

If I could leave you with only one message
It would be: Don't forget to push in your chair
Pick up the papers and garbage from the floor
Say thank you when someone holds the door for you
Smile at that person as you pass them in the hall
Shake firmly, hug often, and kiss...well, when you're ready

I leave you with this message
Not because you have to listen to me
But because you should
My work is out of love
Not money, not power, not because I feel sorry for you
But because I am you
I love you

7TH GRADE ENTRIES

7th grade has been exploring the practice of reflection to promote our growth as community members. We began by defining what reflection means to us — the image in a mirror, thinking about the past and taking personal time. Using our personal definitions, we embarked on a free-writing process, responding to prompts such as, "What inspires you?" "What are you most proud of?" and "What makes you who you are today?" What follows are a few of the poems and prose that emerged from our reflection writings. Thank you for sharing in our dedication to this Guiding Principle. Please enjoy our writing!

By Deana Wojcik, 7th grade Humanities teacher

Something That Makes Me Proud...

By Maria Flores
7th grade

I'm proud of one of the most amazing people that I've ever met, my best friend. My best friend is the best person I've ever had in my life. She is the nicest person that anyone could ever ask for in a friend and a peer. She helps you in everything that she possibly can. If my best friend sees that there is a hungry man standing on the street asking for money, she gives him her lunch even if she does not eat. She is very nice, compassionate, responsible, full of integrity and, most of all; she is one of the smartest people in my school. Even if people take advantage or make fun of her, she doesn't let them hurt her and she always keeps on going. Everyday she comes in with a smile and she is always on task. In her Learning Target grades you will never see anything but "Meets" and "Exceeds". This makes my best friend my idol, my hero and the person I look up to. I am thankful to destiny for putting such a great person in my path and I really believe that Lighthouse is lucky to have this student.

My World: Shaping My Goals and Aspirations

By Fernanda Torres
7th grade

The world I come from
is a world that doesn't give up.
The world I come from
is strong in character.
The world I come from
always helps each other.
The world I come from
always gives me support.
The world I come from
encourages me to do my best
even if it's rough along the way.
The world that I'm talking about is…
My family!

I call this my world because all of my family members together create a strong world. Sometimes people make fun of my birthmark on my forehead. It doesn't bother me, but when they make comments that are more hurtful, I start to care. When people do this to me I use the words of my mother: "You are beautiful and accept yourself the way you are, because God made you like this and you should be proud." Whenever you're down, try saying those words to yourself it really helps. My mom and dad have shown me to respect others and many more things throughout my twelve years of life. My parents always help me to push closer and closer to my dreams. My parents have shown lots of compassion towards me and that has shown me that I really want to be a doctor.

I remember when my mother and I were searching around our closets. It was an event to see! My mother told me about this person who had a family in Guatemala and he needed clothes for his children. My mother and I collected not only clothes, but shoes as well. Everyday we would give him 2–3 big bags filled with clothes and shoes. He also didn't have any money so my dad hired him for work for a couple years. After some time, he left and my family was really sad, because he had become a close friend. Since then, my family cared about him, even though they did not receive anything in return.

This act of kindness has made me care about others as well. My family has taught me to care for others who may not have as much as me. I know that I can support others and I try to do it as often as possible. My family has helped me become the caring person I am today, and I thank them for always caring for me.

8TH GRADE ENTRIES

Lighthouse's 8th grade community focuses on Guiding Principles by exploring them in our advisory program, a dynamic program that addresses character and community development. Some of the highlights from our activities include: a trip to the Oakland Symphony; Crew challenge days in the park; a 3-day camping trip; food and clothing drives; multi-cultural communication simulations and special guest expert musicians and activists. These poets have independently chosen to express their thoughts and feelings about some of the Guiding Principles that resonate with them.

By Kate Parman, 8th grade Humanities teacher

I Miss You

By Henry Huynh
8th grade

I miss you, I miss that friendly smile that made me shed a tear.
I miss you, I miss your expression.
I miss you, even though you're not here with me you'll always be in my heart.
I miss you, but it's time to let you go.
I miss you, I miss seeing you fly.
I miss you, even though you're not here with me I'll always hold you in my arms for eternity.
I miss you, I miss giving you a big friendly hug.
I miss you, even though you're not here with me I can feel you everywhere I go.
I miss you, I miss you even though you're not here with me you'll always be in my heart forever.
I miss you, even though you're not here with me I'll always hold you in my arms for eternity.

Your Life Goals

By Jonté Williams
8th grade

When you're looking for your goals don't ever stop searching, you will find them one day.
And it will give you the right to say, "I've achieved my goals and now I'm so glad.
I finally found my goals that I thought I never had".
See when you don't give up and keep trying your hardest, you will never fail but will go the farthest.
Life is like a big test that you will have to pass in order to succeed, to stay ahead of the class.
There are lots of goals to choose from that you may be interested in, so go out in the world and try your best to win!

I Am

By Arthur Winning
8th grade

I am running
I am dodging blows from a LV.26 siege bug,
slashing open LV.49 zombies,
assassinating LV.20 guardians.
I am running
I am being chased by a LV.15 Harry Potter,
Watching a LV.20 Katrina.
I am running
I am obliterating a 2/4 flying,
desolating a 10/10 indestructible,
incinerating a 60/1 trample.
I am walking
I am with my friends playing games, being my character.
I am still
I am doing my homework
I am awake now
I am

Drip

By Arthur Winning
8th grade

drip drip drip
the sink is broken
drip drip drip
the ghosts of bullies known and friends past
drip drip drip
then I see the ghosts disperse in my mind's eye making way for radiant incorporeal beings
friends still there and true friends who are never lost
squeak squeak
of parents always with us and grandparents we will eventually bury
squeak squeak
the sink is fixed

11TH GRADE ENTRIES

Eleventh grade Humanities students have read, written, and analyzed poems throughout the year. We use our words to express reactions to moments in history, our lives, or share what we know about characters in a novel. As you read our work, you will read about a variety of subjects. Most of all, you will read what we think and how we feel. Thank you for listening to our words and our voices as we share our thoughts with you.

By Drea Beale, 11th grade Humanities teacher

Voting Is Not What It Seems

By Selena Castro
11th grade

The reason I wrote this poem was because it really made me think about how Blacks didn't have the chance to actually vote back in the day. This piece was from a book called, "Freedom Road" and the quotes you see here are parts from different chapters put together so that you can see the vibe I felt about this situation.

"Too many niggers, who thought voting would make them rich, give them the right to speak." "They stared baffled and angry at their empty hands after they had cast their vote". "We prayed, Brother Peter prayed, he prayed to God", "We've done right!" "We're here to learn how to read and we learn how to write, why stop now? Just because we had become like children, ignorant and unknowing, we all just need room to breathe." "We hear someone shout, "NOTIFY, you've been elected!" "Elected? What's that they say, is it power?" "We don't know who the land belongs to, but just maybe it would belong to you and me someday." "But it is the same how men go and spill blood over something like this." "Gideon Jackson, look over there, do you see that? She pointed. Does everybody see that?" "YOU, FREE, YOU'RE FREE, EVERYBODY IS FREE!" "He had never seen those words before, he had NO idea of its meaning."

Brighter Days

By Wendy Diaz
11th grade

As part of a study about voting rights in the United States, 11th grade Humanities students read Howard Fast's "Freedom Road". This historical fiction book chronicles the African-American experience during Reconstruction. The story is told from the perspective of Gideon Jackson, a former slave who is elected a delegate to the South Carolina state legislature. This poem was written as a response to Gideon's joy, fear, and resolve as he voted for the first time.

History has been made once more.
Only this time the road our people have traveled for many years
has become less tedious to travel and become bright with the progression we have made.

The words this man spoke today in his inauguration celebration are the key to the new future this nation holds. "And why a man whose father less than sixty years ago might not have been served at a local restaurant can now stand before you to take a most sacred oath."

I assure you he's correct.
Less than sixty years ago my kids had to attend segregated schools, segregated parks, segregated restaurants, segregated everything.
Thinking back to the great civil rights leaders who sacrificed and stood up for all us colored folks.
I feel that their work and struggles were not in vain.
Now more than ever "I have a dream" has finally turned into reality and actuality.

What seems to keep surprising me nowadays is the leadership and power these young kids have in our country.
My grand kids ain't only worrying about sports, school, and their friends.
They're worrying about how one man can affect their future.
They can choose who they want to lead them.

After this day I feel proud to have lived almost a century in this country.
Seeing all the changes and progression made, I ain't saying this is the beginning of the end but rather he beginning of a new future.

Election Reflection

By Jasmin Dominguez
11th grade

This year Obama and McCain were campaigning against each other for the United States presidency. Both strong debaters, but I believe that Obama was a better and stronger debater. I felt very supportive towards Obama and one of the things I did to show this was to make phone calls. Making phone calls was a good thing to do because many young adults got to be a part of supporting Obama's campaign. I think that I was a responsible and an involved citizen in democracy because my voice was heard while making those phone calls. I felt good helping Obama's campaign and being there was something new to me, because I thought that only adults could do that. I didn't think that they were going to let us teenagers make phone calls, but it was nice of them to let us. The atmosphere of the polling center was very energetic – everybody had a lot of energy moving around and helping each other. I thought that they were very persistent, giving the whole day to make calls just for Obama. Being there made me feel like I had a voice. Even if I didn't make many phone calls, it was fun learning and doing something new. It also made me feel like I was a part of the change this year. This year, democracy taught me that is not easy because when making phone calls, some people were very disrespectful and rude. And you just have to be persistent and not give up just because someone is being disrespectful. If you give up quickly, you are never going to make a change and you are not going to have a voice. Overall, being there was great, I really enjoyed seeing so many people supporting Obama and I enjoyed the fact that they let us be part of that. I know that if Obama were there he would have been proud of them for letting us have a voice and help his campaign. This election year taught me that everybody could be part of democracy; not just adults, but young teenagers, too.

My Understanding

By Maria Hernandez
11th grade

As part of a study about voting rights in the United States, 11th grade Humanities students read Howard Fast's "Freedom Road". This historical fiction book chronicles the African-American experience during Reconstruction. The story is told from the perspective of Gideon Jackson, a former slave who is elected a delegate to the South Carolina state legislature. This poem was written as a response to Gideon's joy, fear, and resolve as he voted for the first time.

This cool November morning, the twenty-seven freedmen came from voting…
but what is this Voting? Brother Peter and my husband Gideon tried to explained it…
"Now that they were freedmen and they had a voice; when there was a matter in question concerning their lives, they used that voice, and that was voting." My husband Gideon told our community what they did when they went to vote… "This here voting's like a wedding or Christmas sermon. Government puts out a strong right arm and says declare yourself. We done that along with five hundred other niggers and white folk, Government says, choose out a delegate…" But what is a Delegate? And Brother Peter said, "We need to pick a man and Gideon's that man… Gideon would go to Charleston and join in the Convention…" Law SAY Black Nigger Man's Free, law SAY Vote, law SAY Niggers man COME OUT OF SLAVERY – *make a life*. That is why niggers' man needs a delegate… now we are coming down freedom road making laws for niggers because now YOU are FREE.

I'm in Control

By Gabriel Huerta
11th grade

I reflect back in the past
And see things gone badly
People die everyday and that's a fact
Not from the nature of earth but the results of the streets
I reflect back in the past
And that is not what I need
I want to succeed in life, and determination is what I need
To accomplish my goals and get out of the streets
Tired of the struggles from the past, now I see the future right in front of me…
The golden door is standing there for me
And I am the only one who holds the key…
I see myself coming out of Lighthouse prepared to succeed to get a degree
I reflect on my past and highlight my mistakes
And make sure that my future life is something I can control

Inauguration Writing Invitation

By Lupita Moreno
11th grade

January 20, 2009 was a huge historical event especially for my people, African Americans. Being an 18-year-old dropout from high school, made me see this day as another chance to change. It was a boost for me to get back into school. Why? Because I thought Blacks couldn't get far in life, since people always say we are all about drugs and the streets. Watching the first African American becoming president in my lifetime, made me reflect on history and on my own mistakes. We as African Americans were once slaves of this country and to see someone my color as a president it's just hard to believe, but really outstanding. Barack Obama is not only an African American, but a well-educated African American man. As I saw him up on stage, watched by billions of people, I was inspired to get back into school, do well, and hopefully become someone like him in life. He inspired me because as he said in his speech, "America is a friend of each nation and every man, woman, and child who seeks a future of peace and dignity..." If it weren't for him, I would've still had the thought that I couldn't become someone important in life because of who I am.

Obama Inauguration Writing Invitation: My Letter to the President

By Juan Carlos Perez
11th grade

Dear Mr. President,
I was once given a writing prompt.
It asked, "What is change?"
With the quickness of an intrigued mind
I reached for a dictionary
It said, "to make the form of something different from what it is"
I pulled my nose out of that book
On my face, a confused and pensive look
Because according to this text, that's all that it took.

Dear Mr. President,
You've made it clear that we all have our part
You've opened our minds and entered our hearts
You've said change isn't easy and I understand what you said
You won't rule this nation and we'll help you instead

Dear Mr. President,
You stood tall and proud
And you didn't allow
Us to bow down, to the irresponsible crowd
That's been in the White House for these past *eight years*

Dear Mr. President,
You've not only handed the Rope
To connect us as a Nation
But you've giving us the Hope
To move away from this political segregation

Dear Mr. President,
I stood in awe of this question
It didn't allow me to rest and
I finally walked back to this prompt
That asked, "What is change?"
And I put under it was Obama '08

Changes

By Ana Rivas
11th grade

Students in 11th grade Humanities were encouraged and inspired by the election and inauguration of President Barack Obama. In response to an invitation to write about the inauguration speech, Ana Rivas wrote this short narrative from the perspective of a young woman in college. Enjoy!

Ring ring... wake up mom it's time to go and receive the new president and welcome him to Washington, D.C. where he's going to be in the White House. "Mom, are you going to be ready in 10 minutes?" "Yes, I will," said my mom. "We are going to be on our way." I was so excited that I told my mom, "Wow mom you can see people from far away!" "There are more than a million people here to receive him." My heart wanted to jump out of the happiness I was knowing that today, January 20, 2009, the new President Obama is going to be here in the White House making changes for the world. "Wow, you hear that mom, he said there's going to be changes in our world and we are going to change it for better." "Yes, I heard that." "Wow, I have hope in Obama that he's going to be the best president and he's going to make changes for people by creating more jobs like he said in his speech, you hear that?" "Yes, I heard that." "Did you also hear he said that we have chosen hope over fear?" "Yes, I heard that too." Now Obama's Inauguration was over we were on the way home. As we were going on our way home in our car I was talking to my mom about the changes Obama is going to make.

One change I think will be that there is going to be more jobs for people. If that change happens then I can see myself changing to a different job that pays me more than the job I have right now. Today there is a crisis with money. Like people trying to pay for their homes and pay their telephone and water bills. Many changes are coming in our world and we as people are going to make changes in our world for the better with President Obama. We are going to have challenges but we as a people are not going to give up easily and will fight for our rights with the support of Obama.

I'm Proud To Be Brown

By Isidro Ruvalcaba
11th grade

Oakland youth,
going to college can be a sacrifice,
so you'll have to speak the truth.
Don't let anyone put you down,
no matter if you're Black, Asian, or brown.
College is a great accomplishment in life,
gangs are not because sooner or later,
you'll get stabbed with a pocketknife.
No matter where you're from,
college can accept you,
even if you think you're dumb.
Lighthouse guides you with a glowing bright light,
follow it and you will succeed even if you're not white.
So my people of many colors,
apply to as many scholarships as possible,
because they could choose you as a winner,
to pay for college with thousands of dollars.

Santiago's Election Reflection

By Santiago Villalba
11th grade

There are a couple of ways that show that I am responsible and an involved citizen in our democracy. One way was by going with my teacher and classmates to the Obama campaign call center to make phone calls to the battleground states. In order for me to do this, I got a list of people and phone numbers to call. I called people in Ohio and Pennsylvania to remind them to go vote for Obama or to tell them where their polling place was located. There were different kinds of people. Some people were nice and had positive comments while others had negative comments. There were people that would say, "Thank you for the reminder, I already voted for Obama" or "I will be voting later tonight, thank you." Some people with negative comments would say things like, "Quit f****** calling me!" or "Who is this, can you stop calling me s***. I don't got time for all this and I already voted for McCain." I didn't reply back to people with the negative attitude. I would end each call saying, "Thank you for your time and have a good day." The atmosphere in the polling center was really exciting and focused. People were really happy to make phone calls to help Obama. Also, a lot of people came out to help make phone calls. The goal was to make a thousand calls in one hour. Everybody was really focused making the calls. People were doing what they were supposed to do and answering any questions people would ask of them. Being in the phone center made me feel part of the Obama campaign. I felt a part of all this because I was actually calling people to remind them to go vote for Obama. My work was part of the democratic process because I was trying to help Obama get people to vote for him. I learned from this experience that if you want to make a change then people should get together and work together. Also that everyone has put in some kind of effort to accomplish what they want.

Dreams & Hopes

By Michael Zepeda
11th grade

I have a Dream
that this nation will rise up and live
that we will be transformed into an oasis of freedom and justice
that we will not be judged by the color of skin but our character
I have a Dream

I Know
that we need change
that we the American people upon which this nation relies on
that our challenge may be new
that we have gathered because we have chosen hope over fear
I Know

I Hope
to get along
to fix our mistakes
to be fair
to have peace
I Hope

12TH GRADE ENTRIES

Over the course of the past several months, the seniors of Lighthouse Community Charter School have been engaged in many studies of human rights, individual identity, patterns of change in the world and self-expression through poetry. The seniors wrote poetry in reaction to events in their lives, memories that they cherish, people they love and honor and emotions that needed a voice. In the following pages, you are invited to share their perspectives and visions. These poems represent some of the many voices of our first graduating class of 2009. As they go on to college and beyond, they take with them a hope for change and an understanding of the power of language.

By Yael Irom, 12th grade Humanities teacher

Take It Easy, Ma

By Angelica Cuevas
12th grade

Take it easy, Ma
Just sit down and relax
Don't put too much on your shoulders
Let it all pass

Let it rest
Let it settle
Leave it all in God's hands
Don't let anything bring you down

Take it easy, Ma
Don't rush things
They will be okay
Just sit down and relax

Believe it or not
I appreciate you
I appreciate everything you do for us

But remember,
Take it easy, Ma
I will be okay
I know how to handle things
I know my way

Take it easy, Ma
There's no time to rush
There's no time to stress
There's no time for games

We love you
We appreciate you
So take it easy, Ma

Dead Memories

By Eulises Esquivel
12th grade

Little boy cries,
Dead memories,
The boy sees his grandma die,
Dead memories,
The little boy at the playground grieving,
Dead memories,
The boy thinks the world has no meaning,
Dead memories,
The boy is lonely watching his friends with their parents,
Dead memories,
He watches them all go away,
Dead memories,
The boy watches his mother's tears roll down her cheeks,
Dead memories,
She's hiding something covert, something she wishes not to reveal,
Dead memories,
Now, 17, the mother tells the boy the secret.
The boy looks at his dad,
How they look so unlike,
And he realizes the truth.
Nothing but dead memories.

Something New

By Jasmine Jenkins
12th grade

I see round brown amber eyes staring back into my eyes.
I smell strong men's cologne.
I hear words silently coming from his lips.
I feel warm hands within my hands.
A cold breeze wraps around my little hips.
I taste starburst candy green apple flavor.
I think I'm happy again.

Right Here In the Town

By German Lopez
12th grade

I fell in love with cars right here in the town.

Right here in the town
The roar of an engine shows no fear to its competition.

Right here in the town
People slang and bang.

Right here in the town
In every corner you hear the sound of tires peeling out.

Right here in the town
At midnight, people show off their skills behind the wheel.

Right here in the town
The sound of gunshots can go off at any moment.

Right here in the town
You see baby mamas in Hondas.

Right here in the town

People in the town must watch their own back anywhere they go.
Right here in the town
Right here in the town
Right here in the town!

One Mirror

By Tania Maldonado
12th grade

One mirror is all I need…
  To see past smiles
  To peek at the future
  To ask my other side
  To seek for answers
One mirror is all I need…
  To imagine what could be
  To see the opposite perspectives
  Of my own mind's views
One mirror is all I need…
  To catch reflection
  My reflection
One mirror is all I need…
  To know there's more to what we see

I Don't Understand

By Janae Miller
12th grade

I don't understand...
Why there's global warming
Why flamingos are pink
Why we always assume that we have all the time in the world to get things done

But most of all...
Why there are genocides all over the world
Why police are so unfair
Why food is so scarce in Africa
Why rappers look down on women

What I understand most is...
Why students deserve to have an education
Why Barack Obama is our president
Why it's imperative to get tested
Why college plays a huge role in life

Because We See...

By Janae Miller
12th grade

Because we see obstacles, we don't see persistence
Because we see racism, we don't see Civil War
Because we see money, we don't see the failure of the economy
Because we see gangs, we don't see the homicide rate
Because we see burgers and fries, we don't see obesity
Because we see school, we don't see a brighter future
Because we see ourselves, we don't see community
Because we see relationships, we don't see real love
Because we see equity, we don't see equality
Because we see designer clothes, but we don't see child labor
Because we see police brutality, we don't see genocides
Because we see what we want to see, we don't see the world

It Took a Tear

By Victor Peña
12th grade

It took a tear,
To recognize my mistake
Of becoming a failure
It took a tear,
To value my father for all his hard work
It took a tear,
To be in love with Vianey
It took a tear,
To leave the streets cuz I saw so many lose their lives
It took a tear,
To express my feelings cuz I never do
It took a tear,
To lose her cuz she meant more than a girlfriend
It took a tear,
To say goodbye to my mom cuz it's the first time I lost something special
It took a tear,
Trying to regain her love but it seems not to work
It took a tear,
Trying to accept the truth, but I can't
It took a tear,
To cry cuz men don't cry
It took a tear,
To bring her in my life cuz she was the "One"
It took a tear,
To bring her up cuz it still burns
Finally, it took a tear,
To write this poem cuz poems are for girls

Karina

By Hector Ramirez
12th grade

Her eyes squint, her voice giggles.
Innocent secrets revealed through the
pencil containing flakes of every color.
She was next to me.
Still, sitting on her chair.
No worry in mind, no recess in her mind.

My knees were an inch from her toes.
With the grace of a rose petal,
I touched her face.
Warmth radiated from the smile
that I kissed.

The teacher looked.
Everyone looked.
No one moved.

Then, they continued with their lives.
So did she.
So did I.

When I Think of Poetry

By Adriana Ramos
12th grade

I think of love, pain, joy, hate.
I think of red, pink, blue, and violet.
I think of shoes, bras, and nail polish.
I think of pens, pencils, and paper.
I think of dreams, hope, and failures.
I think of tears, knives, and clouds.
I think of black, blue, ink.
... I think of imagination.
I think of poems.

I Got My Hair Cut, I Hope He Likes It

By Adriana Ramos
12th grade

Short chocolate brown hair hugs my rounded cheeks.
I shyly glide into Six Silver Stars from the far left corner,
Imagining what he would say, "You're really cute, I love your smile."
My desk is the light at the end of the tunnel. Never nearing.
The windows trap rays of sunlight. Spring heat embraces my body.
Joy lifts the corners of my lips.
"I hope he likes it, I hope he likes it."
He exists. No one else.
His hair stands like gelled soldiers.
His uniform clings loosely to his lanky frame.
The sun disappears.
A gray blanket covers the classroom.
Blurred memory, slow motion.
My stomach back flips, butterflies get hectic.
I hug my sweater.
Self-consciousness creeps into my mind.
Heat climbs up my face, settling down.
My smile disappears into nothing.
It was a stupid schoolgirl crush.
Others notice, not him.
I got my hair cut in sixth grade...
I hope he likes it.

The Place Where I Want To Be

By Mayra Salcido
12th grade

The place where I want to be is somewhere where the crisp cold weather constantly embraces everyone and politely embellishes its surroundings with delicate white petals of snow laying on the ground untouched.

A place where the sun's rays are not frequent visitors.
A place where the night stays still, while serenity takes over the deep blue skies.
A place where the road to success is endless and full of intriguing possibilities.
A place where numerous opportunities are waiting to be fulfilled.
A place where at the end of the day I can call home.

This is where I want to be.

A Masked Mannequin

By Elise Sien
12th grade

Skinny.
Luscious Hair
Cherry Lips
Barbie Hips
It sways,
side
to side
walks with grace
with her porcelain face
o, the way she speaks   &
o, her body is so sleek   &
o,   perfection she is   &
o, how she is all his &
o,   lovely she is   &
it is all a lie
no one could have
seen right through her
pain and her bitter eyes
no one could have known
that her past was just so cold
but she hides it so well behind
her smile
her laugh
her grace
she is a
masked mannequin

Today's Smile

By Vianey Servin
12th grade

When tears dry and words fail,
Today's smile.
The explanation I never received,
Today's smile.
The rose that never bloomed,
Today's smile.
The two years we could have shared,
Today's smile.
The joy in your face that I'll never see again,
Today's smile.
The Hawaii trip that will never happen,
Today's smile.
The toe I never iced,
Today's smile.
The medication I never followed,
Today's smile.
The pain I seem to forget,
Today's smile.
The lesson that I never learned,
Today's smile.
The tear I can't take back,
Today's smile.
The apology that I cannot accept,
Today's smile.
The erasable moments within my head,
Today's smile.
Today's smile.
Yesterday's heartbreak,
Tomorrow's happiness,
Today's smile.

Rain

By Vianey Servin
12th grade

I see the clouds forming,
I smell the breeze of water,
I hear the birds crying,
I feel the drops of pain,
I taste the moist of the air,
I think it's going to rain.

I Am

By Perla Topete
12th grade

I am confident and strong
I wonder what the future holds for me
I hear the constant reminder that "Time is running out!"
I see time fly by
I want to make the right decisions
I am confident and strong

I pretend I don't need any help
I feel crippled by the idea of failure
I touch the ropes tying me down
I worry about hurting others and hurting myself
I CRY
I am confident and strong

I understand that sometimes I won't do what's right
I say everything will be fine
I dream of everything being fine
I try to make everything fine
I HOPE
I am confident and strong!

Love at First Sight

By Aunnamarie Viceral
12th grade

A GLANCE
You caught me off guard
I watched you from the corner of my eye
A NOTICE
I hesitate to speak
Lost for words to my surprise
A CALL
Kind of flattered
Still don't have much to say
A TEXT
Still contemplating
I'll wait for one more day
A PARTY
There you go, re-capturing my eye
All of a sudden, I have butterflies
A TOUCH
My body tingles
My mind escapes to cloud nine
A KISS
My feelings erupt
My heart and mind intertwine.

The City Life

By Mayra Salcido, Breyana Riley, Veronica Garcia Guzman and Yasmin Guerrero
12th grade

Black and white suits with blank faces adorn the mundane sidewalks under
the scorching sunlight.
Newspaper pages dance at the scent of fresh brewed coffee.
Beep! Beep! Taxis honk through the congested traffic, creating the soundtrack of the
everyday rush hour.
As the sun gets ready to greet the night, suits are put away and the Nightlife rejuvenates.
Swirls of perfume conquer the streets and glistening glowing glitter announces the
glamorous city life.

I Am From

By Janet Tillman
Dean of Students

I am from a state that hasn't embraced or accepted our oneness.
I am from a city that continues to struggle to reinvent itself.
I am from a community whose members are taught to advocate for themselves.
I am from a profession that has the privilege to stretch and grow with young people.
I am from an administration that models our 10 Guiding Principles.
I am from a staff that is committed to serving the whole student.
I am from a group of students who have experienced devastating challenges.
I am from students who know and live diversity everyday.
I am from students who love deeply and express themselves courageously.
I am from a hope that all Lighthouse students will become resilient adults.
I am from a heart that pains to say good-bye.

Printed in the United States
by Baker & Taylor Publisher Services